VOLUME 2

MAD WITH WONDER

Dedicated to the lost Sir Cook,
following his own radical map

Hatter
VOLUME 2
MAD WITH WONDER

Written by Frank Beddor & Liz Cavalier
Art by Sami Makkonen

AUTOMATIC
PICTURES
PUBLISHING

Hatter M: Mad With Wonder
Volume 2

Writers
Frank Beddor
Liz Cavalier

Art
Sami Makkonen

Cover Art
Tae Young Choi

Letterer
Tom B. Long

Editor
C.J. Wrobel

Reconnaissance & Analysis
Nate Barlow

Civil War Raconteur
Miss Emily McGuiness

Logo Designed by
Christina Craemer

Interiors Designed by
Vera Milosavich

Institute Artists
Chris Appelhans
Catia Chien
Tae Young Choi
Brian Flora
Vance Kovacs

www.lookingglasswars.com

Excerpts from *ArchEnemy: The Looking Glass Wars, Book Three* used with
permission of Penguin Books for Young Readers. All rights reserved.

From *Princess Alyss of Wonderland* by Frank Beddor, illustrated by Catia
Chien and Vance Kovacs, Copyright © 2007 by Frank Beddor. Used by
permission of Dial Books for Young Readers, A Division of Penguin Young
Readers Group, A Member of Penguin Group (USA) Inc., 345 Hudson
Street, New York, NY 10014. All rights reserved

Printed in Korea

ISBN 978-0-9818737-2-5

This is ~~not~~ the story
of a Mad Hatter

Thank You

Scholars, Antiquarians,
Reasoners, Logicians, Rationalists,
and Knights Errant

Contents

Sami's Imagination at Work

Introduction

Much like Royal Bodyguard Hatter Madigan, I too have been on a non-stop quest following the Glow of Imagination. The object of my search was not, however, a lost princess but the artist to whom Ben Templesmith would pass the hallowed scepter of visual documentation. For over a year I trekked across continents in the hope of finding the paint-stained partner that would illustrate the volume you now hold in your hands. I did not limit my search to celebrated schools or established professionals but instead wandered the alleys claimed by Rio de Janeiro's muralists and the unmarked galleries of Shanghai looking for the *ONE*. Finally, exhausted and disillusioned, I was about to return to Los Angeles when I received a cryptic email from Joe Pruett of Desperado Comics. The email contained only the latitude and longitude of a small town in Finland and the name *Sami Makkonen*. Boarding a plane at midnight for the redeye to Finland I had a premonition that within hours I would be seated at a café table with the artist who would illustrate geo-graphic novel Hatter M Volume 2. My second sight proved correct and for the next several weeks Sami and I sat together at a scarred table in a forgotten café debating and analyzing the visuals that would bring this volume to life. I would watch as Sami intuitively pulled colors from the Wonderland spectrum and mixed them with his Finnish sensibility for an inter-realm artistry and silently marvel at my good fortune in finding one so talented and Imaginative! Thanks to Joe Pruett and Sami Makkonen I am now able to share with you Volume 2 of Hatter M's search — *Mad with Wonder*.

Frank Beddor

"In a completely sane world, madness is the only freedom!" –J. G. BALLARD

"We are all born mad. Some remain so." –SAMUEL BECKETT

Prologue

THAT IMAGINATION BELONGS TO ME!

ALL IMAGINATION BELONGS TO ME. IF THIS DRAINING IS POSSIBLE I WILL DRAIN EVERY LAST BIT OF IMAGINATION AND RETURN IT TO WONDERLAND. MY INVENTORS AND ALCHEMISTS WILL FIND A WAY...

...OR ELSE FACE THE CONSEQUENCES.

YOU TWO. FIND THOSE ON EARTH WITH DARK MORALITY AND GREED FOR MATERIAL GAIN. RECRUIT THEM TO ACT AS MY OPERATIVES.

We will do anything for the cause of Black Imagination~ but what about the bodyguard?

HE'S LOST... ALL WHO LEAVE WONDERLAND AND TRAVEL BEYOND THE POOL OF TEARS ARE LOST. IF ANY COULD RETURN...

...THEY WOULD HAVE. HATTER MADIGAN'S SEARCH IS MADNESS. THE PRINCESS IS LONG DEAD.

Imperfect...I wander an imperfect world in search of
Alyss. Daunting and vast.
197 million square miles...70.8% aqua...29.2%
terra.
If not for the Glow that appears to beckon and guide
me I would be as lost as she. How can one so small
have a mission so great? One by one...doors keep
opening...and I must carry on.

"Anybody remotely interesting is mad, in some way or another." —DOCTOR WHO

Timbromania

A Flying Cloud transports me to the Land of
Opportunity. The people say anything is possible
there. That anything you can dream can be made
manifest. Is America this world's Wonderland?

"The worst of madmen is a saint run mad." —ALEXANDER POPE

Amazing Grace

ATLANTIC OCEAN, 1864

You believe this sort of thing?

angel of the Battlefield – Witnesses at the bloody battlefields
the American Civil War have sworn to the presence of a young girl
veloped in an unearthly glow who comforts the injured
nd dying soldiers of both the North and the South...

I do.

Me too!
We HAVE to
believe. In this
brutal world it's
all we have.
Ain't it?

50

Welcome all ye faithful! I trust the force of goodness has brought you all here tonight to witness the miracle that is among us...

Will those here to be healed please come forward to meet Sister Sally.

Sister Sally's apostles will now pass amongst you, please give generously, so that the miracles may begin...

Amen!

PIFF POP

GADZOOKS! That's...

BZZZZZSHRRNNNG

You'll all be home real soon now.

If your girl isn't with the others then Van De Skulle has already taken her up to the mirror room.

Why?

To sell her soul. Before the war Van De Skulle sold slaves— now he sells souls.

Who's out there?!

I got two shotguns and a nervous twitch!

HATTER MADIGAN

Civil War in Wonderland...Civil War in America.
What world doesn't have war? Someday I should
like to travel there and perhaps...retire.

"The great proof of madness is the disproportion of one's designs to one's means." –NAPOLEON BONAPARTE

J.A. Early

BY LATE SUMMER IN 1864,
AMERICA'S CIVIL WAR HAD
ENTERED ITS FINAL HORRIFIC
YEAR. AS THE UNION FORCES
CONTINUED TO GAIN
CONFEDERACY TERRITORY,
GENERAL ROBERT LEE
ASSIGNED THE PUGNACIOUS
LT. GENERAL JUBAL A. EARLY
(NICKNAMED OLD JUBILEE)
TO SWEEP THE YANKEES
FROM THE SHENANDOAH
VALLEY IN VIRGINIA AND TO
MENACE WASHINGTON D.C. BY
OCTOBER OF 1864 EARLY'S
FORCES HAD FOUGHT SEVERAL
BATTLES COMING CLOSE
TO TAKING WASHINGTON BUT
WITHOUT SUCCESS.

THE BATTLE OF CEDAR CREEK
(OCTOBER 19, 1864) WOULD
PROVE A DEFINITIVE TURNING
POINT IN THE WAR... AND
PSYCHE... OF THIS WILDCAT
CONFEDERATE WARRIOR.

Look out,
Mr. Lincoln...
I'm a comin' to
Washington.

CHOOSING BOLDNESS,
OLD JUBILEE PLANNED
AN ASSAULT ON THE
SUPERIOR UNION FORCES,
USING SURPRISE TO HIS
ADVANTAGE. HE DEPLOYED
HIS MEN IN THREE COLUMNS
IN AN AUDACIOUS NIGHT
MARCH, LIGHTED ONLY
BY THE MOON.

JUST BEFORE SUNRISE,
OPERATING UNDER A
COVER OF DENSE FOG,
THE CONFEDERATES
ATTACKED. THE SURPRISE
WAS COMPLETE.

HUNDREDS OF UNION
PRISONERS WERE
TAKEN, MANY OF
THEM STILL IN THEIR
BEDCLOTHES.

AS SHERIDAN AND OTHER DIVISIONS ENGAGED THE UNPREPARED CONFEDERATE TROOPS, GENERAL CUSTER'S CAVALRY UNIT DESTROYED A BRIDGE IN THE CONFEDERATE REAR, CUTTING OFF THEIR ESCAPE ROUTE. MANY OF THE VETERAN SOUTHERN TROOPS SURRENDERED, CERTAIN THEY COULD NOT FIGHT THEIR WAY OUT OF THE DEBACLE.

THE BATTLE OF CEDAR CREEK HAD ENDED IN HUMILIATING DEFEAT FOR LT. GENERAL JUBAL A. EARLY.

How many?

How many... what?

I asked you, Doctor Stoker. How many DEAD?! How many WOUNDED?!

Now is not the time to speak of the dead and wounded. Now is the time to consider the LIVING!

I fear I feel too much. Emotions are inappropriate to my sworn duty. And yet...I feel love and loss and rage and...fear. What does a bodyguard become who has given up the right to feel?

"Love is merely madness..." — WILLIAM SHAKESPEARE

Love & Death

101

117

My name is Hatter Mad...Mad...Madigan...

"The only difference between me and a madman is that I am not mad." —SALVADOR DALI

Asylum

122

123

Hat's free!

Aloft without the heaviness of consciousness.
No guilt propels me.

No loss haunts.

Hat is no longer separated from life by the
call of duty.

Hat flies free and soars knowing that moment
by moment…

Hat will be led back to him.

"A breath of wind from the wings of madness." —CHARLES BAUDELAIRE

Hats Off!

143

145

147

I have learned that my search is not just the route
I follow but includes those individuals I encounter.
Each…if I choose to listen…has a word that will
assist me. My search will end in success when I am
able to put all of their words together.

"Madness need not be all breakdown. It may also be break-through. It is potential liberation and renewal as well as enslavement and existential death." – R. D. Laing

Revelation

Is my search in vain?

You must learn to travel in a certain direction rather than striving for an end-point which does not exist.

Is Alyss alive?!

Not as she once was.

WHERE IS SHE?!

If anyone knows where Alyss is it's the United States Government. All the secrets are kept in Washington D.C.

155

157

159

161

163

IN MARCH OF 1865, GENERAL LEE RELIEVED LT. GENERAL JUBAL EARLY OF HIS COMMAND. CONCERNED BY HIS RECENT ACTIONS, LEE DOUBTED EARLY'S ABILITY TO INSPIRE CONFIDENCE IN THE MEN HE WOULD HAVE TO RECRUIT TO CONTINUE OPERATIONS. HE WROTE TO EARLY OF THE DIFFICULTY OF THIS DECISION:

While my own confidence in your ability, zeal, and devotion to the cause is unimpaired

General Lee has lost faith in me.

I have failed the South. I have failed myself.

You are too valuable to fail.

What are you saying?

You swore to burn Washington And you will.

How?

By using... imagination.

Her Imperial Viciousness is eager to drain this leader named Lincoln.

Don't disappoint her.

I wouldn't dream of it.

167

Enjoy a sneak preview of
Hatter M Volume 3

*Translated from Morse Code:
"Priority one. Dead rebel."

173

Hatter M

INSTITUTE FOR PARANORMAL

Take a moment and breathe deeply, we believe there is much to absorb from the preceding pages brought to you at the speed of Imagination. Researching, writing, illustrating and assembling geo-graphic novel *Hatter M: Mad with Wonder, Volume 2*, was an epic task for all of us here at the Institute. We chose to focus on the pivotal time period of 1864 – 1865 for Hatter's travels because in the course of our research we came upon several pieces of the intricate puzzle that forms the basis of the Looking Glass Wars saga.

Beginning with chapter one we delved headlong into one of the most quotidian of mysteries. How did Royal Bodyguard Hatter Madigan finance his extensive travels for 13 years? Through the excellent sleuthing of our London office, headed by Dame Agnes MacKenzie, we were able to uncover the seemingly insignificant Sir Lucius Oliphant Wellesley. Wellesley's unabashed timbromania (if you haven't checked your French dictionary by now it is a mania for stamp collecting) as the geographical impetus for his occasional funding of Hatter's travels was verified by cross-referencing his stamp collection with Hatter's journal and other travel ephemera including tickets and maps.

If the location of a stamp coveted by Wellesley coincided with Hatter's Glow ordained destination a deal would be struck whereupon Hatter's travel expenses would be paid in return for his assistance in procuring the desired stamp. This gentlemen's agreement was in itself fortuitous, but when Dame Agnes discovered that Sir Wellesley's full name was actually 'George Lucius Oliphant Wellesley' a whole other dimension of speculation opened given his initials now spelled G.L.O.W.! Dame Agnes has been an indispensable contributor to the Institute. As you turn a few more pages you will find an excerpt from her book, *Princess Alyss of Wonderland*, the art and letters from the lost journals of Princess Alyss Heart during her exile in our world.

Hatter's decision to follow the glow to the battlefields of the American Civil War led the Institute's Miss Emily

TRAVEL

and Colonel Barlow on a merry chase through dusty antebellum archives researching Lt. General Jubal Early's obsessive fixation to invade Washington D.C. How Early and Hatter's paths collided in our nation's capital will be revealed in Hatter M Volume 3. But it was Hatter's stay at the West Virginia Hospital for the Insane that provided the most astounding revelation of all! Given access to the asylum's vaults, Colonel Barlow came upon a crumbling intake file dated March 1865 and labeled 'Mad Man X'. Upon opening the file he was rewarded with the details of Hatter's incarceration including Dr. Frood's notes on his mental state and prescribed treatment.

But surely the most startling find of all was an illustrated card tucked inside the file and matching the style and artistry of the illuminated deck of Wonderland cards that first inspired Frank Beddor's investigation into the Looking Glass Wars! The card found in the file has been meticulously carbon tested and verified as the missing link that finally answers the question of who was the creator of The Looking Glass Wars deck of cards. We can now accurately state that the artist was Royal Bodyguard Hatter Madigan. Turn the page to see this pivotal piece of history and the newest card of the H.A.T.B.O.X.

With the genesis of the deck now in our sights we will continue to track the paper trail of the Looking Glass Wars cards and how they came to be in the possession of both the British Museum and antiquities dealer Mr. Buffington.

As a final note, dear reader, we hope you will share news of geo-graphic novel *Hatter M: Mad With Wonder, Volume 2*, with other dedicated followers of White Imagination as you prepare your psyches for the further adventures of Hatter M in the forthcoming Volume 3. Thank you for continuing to join us in following the glow!

The Hatter M Institute for Paranormal Travel

Hospital for the Insane

The West Virginia Hospital for the Insane (currently known as the Weston State Hospital and declared a national historic landmark) has proven to be one our most fascinating discoveries. Colonel Barlow spent weeks combing through the remains of this crumbling, massive example of Gothic Revival architecture. In the course of his search he came upon a storeroom filled with rotting furniture, seemingly undisturbed since the days of the Civil War. In a roll top desk he found a newspaper article and photograph torn from the Weston Gazette dated April 1st, 1865. From what we can glean

PERRINE'S NEW MILITARY MAP ILLUSTRATING THE SEAT OF WAR

SOUTHERN PART OF FLORIDA

Hatter's Map to the Asylum

WESTON GAZETTE • April 1, 1865

BINGO! DR. FROOD WINS AGAIN!

from the text of the badly damaged article there was a period of several weeks following Dr. Frood's nervous breakdown when an acting superintendent arrived and took over the asylum. The gazette reports that 'Dr. Elijah Von Wonder' not only took over the day to day management of the asylum but during his brief stay implemented humane and enlightened practices that continue to influence psychiatric therapy today. At this time we do not know where 'Dr. Elijah Von Wonder' went after he left the asylum but rest assured we are investigating and will have updates in the near future.

"Madness in great ones must not unwatched go." –WILLIAM SHAKESPEARE

Floorplan of the West Virginia Hospital for the Insane

HOSPITAL FOR THE INSANE

The lunatic asylum that housed Royal Bodyguard Hatter Madigan for several weeks in March 1865 still stands today in Weston, West Virginia. Tours of the asylum offering firsthand access to paranormal sightings (ghosts!) are open to the public.

177

Mystery Solved

"I'd rather be mad with the truth than sane with lies." —An anonymous psychiatric patient and poet

Behold…the lost card. This card is the link connecting the Wonderland cards discovered by Frank Beddor in the British Museum and the deck collected by British antiquities dealer Mr. Buffington with Hatter Madigan, royal bodyguard and artist. For reasons unknown, this card depicting Wonderland's Millinery H.A.T.B.O.X. remained at the asylum while the other cards were moved. We wonder how many cards are in this deck and if any are still missing. How and why did the existing deck travel to England? Questions… questions. Evidently the mystery is not solved but more tantalizing. We will continue to search for other missing cards depicting as yet unseen images of Wonderland and share our discoveries in geographic novel Hatter M Volume 3.

We hope you enjoy the color art images inspired by Hatter Madigan's cards and rendered by our very own Institute artists.

HATBOX

H.A.T.B.O.X.: Holographic and Transmutative
Base of Xtremecombat: High vibrational
training facility for Millinery Bodyguards.

Now, after nearly 150 years, the cards can be
reunited in their original box.

QUEEN REDD

THE CAT

A PRINCESS ALYSS

Queen Genevieve

THE CHESSBOARD DESERT

VALLEY OF MUSHROOMS

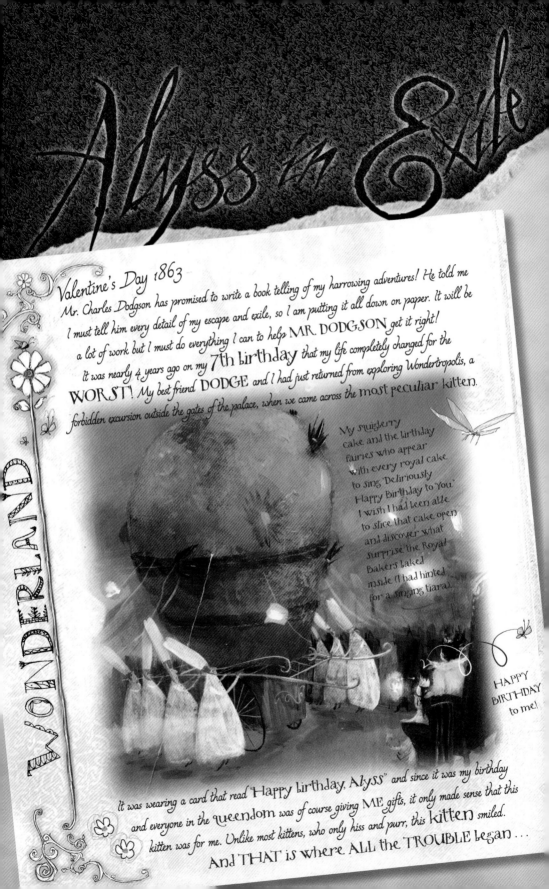

Alyss in Exile

WONDERLAND

Valentine's Day 1863

Mr. Charles Dodgson has promised to write a book telling of my harrowing adventures! He told me I must tell him every detail of my escape and exile, so I am putting it all down on paper. It will be a lot of work but I must do everything I can to help MR. DODGSON get it right!

It was nearly 4 years ago on my 7th birthday that my life completely changed for the WORST! My best friend DODGE and I had just returned from exploring Wondertropolis, a forbidden excursion outside the gates of the palace, when we came across the most peculiar kitten.

My squiglerry cake and the birthday fairies who appear with every royal cake to sing "Deliriously Happy Birthday to You." I wish I had been able to slice that cake open and discover what surprise the Royal Bakers baked inside (I had hinted for a singing tiara).

HAPPY BIRTHDAY to me!

It was wearing a card that read "Happy birthday, Alyss" and since it was my birthday and everyone in the Queendom was of course giving ME gifts, it only made sense that this kitten was for me. Unlike most kittens, who only hiss and purr, this kitten smiled.

And THAT is where ALL the TROUBLE began . . .

Charles Dodgson's aptitude in the nascent art of photography made him a popular portraitist of children for Oxford's better families. Choosing their costumes for the various portraits was always left to the girls, and might I suggest that the photograph of Alyss in the white dress appears to be her tribute to her time spent with Quigley and the others as a street urchin. It is interesting to note that Charles Dodgson's custom of marking dates of great importance with a white stone may well have stemmed from the Wonderland custom.

Charles Dodgson at age 25 photographed by Reginald Southey.

Monday Morning

I mark the date April 1, 1862 with a white stone, for it is when I first met Mr. Charles Dodgson! (In **Wonderland** it is custom to always mark days of great imagination with a white stone. When we were introduced I looked up and saw the kindest face I had seen since leaving Wonderland. I liked him **immediately** but it wasn't until Lorina introduced me very grandly as Princess Alyss Heart (mocking me, of course) that I knew he was to be my **best friend** in this world, for the man bowed quite seriously, took my hand and **whispered**, "Delighted to make your acquaintance, **Princess Alyss Heart**"

Alice as a beggar maid.

Alice photographed by Dodgson.

Tuesday

Soon after our introduction Mr. Dodgson invited Lorina, Edith and me to his studio for our first photographic portrait. What we all enjoyed most about the portrait setting was being able to try on the costumes that Mr. Dodgson had collected. I told him that I had not seen such imaginative **costumes** since I left Wonderland. He became very interested and said he would like to hear more about this **land** called **Wonderland**.

CDL

Dear Princess Alyss Heart,

I would be most honored if you and your sisters Lorina and Edith would join me for a day of boating and picnicking along the Thames. I am looking forward to hearing all about this world you call Wonderland.

Inquisitively yours,
Charles Lutwidge Dodgson

After the publication of the Looking Glass Wars, we were contacted by the British historian Dame Agnes Mackenzie who had some very interesting information to share. A trunk had been discovered inside a dilapidated carriage house in Oxford, England. It contained the art and journals of a young Victorian girl. After an intensive examination we confirmed the contents to be the property of Princess Alyss Heart of Wonderland. Alyss' art, letters and journal entries provide a haunting portal into the mind of a lost princess searching for a way home. Dame Agnes' book *Princess Alyss of Wonderland* beautifully displays Alyss' work along with her own meticulously researched notes and annotations to provide the reader with historical background and commentary. The excerpted pages follow the trajectory of Alyss and Lewis Carroll's great friendship, the collaboration on the promised book and the ultimate literary betrayal that forever separated muse and author. As The Looking Glass Wars first revealed, Lewis Carroll got it all wrong.

"Oh, you can't help that," said the cat. "We're all mad here." —LEWIS CARROLL

"But I don't want to go among mad people," said Alice.

26 November 1864

In November of 1864, Charles Dodgson proudly and dare I venture, a bit shyly, presented "Miss Alice Liddell" with his handwritten manuscript of ALICE'S ADVENTURES UNDERGROUND. This historic manuscript contained 37 illustrations also drawn by the versatile and prolific Mr. Dodgson. As you shall SOON DISCOVER, Alyss' reaction was not quite what the poor man had anticipated!

And at long last the promised book was delivered. What can I say?
HE GOT IT ALL WRONG
WRONG WRONG WRONG WRONG!!!!
He even spelled my name *wrong! What makes me want to scream* off with his head AND *both arms is the fact that he actually seems to believe* HE told ME *this nonsensical children's story when the truth is (and he knows it!) that* I told him.

To the Very CRUEL Mr. Dodgson,

How could you betray me with this pack of lies? If I were not so furious with you I would certainly be sobbing at the loss of what I believed to be my one true friend in this gray world. Be warned, for the sake of Wonderland and everyone I love, I cannot allow this book of lies to go unchallenged. And who is this "Lewis Carroll" that you are now calling yourself? Are you ashamed to put your own name on this book? I should hope so! As if a royal princess would ever travel through a rabbit hole! Thanks to your efforts my reality has now become this world's fantasy.

Your Un-Friend,
Princess Alyss Heart

PS. Now you shall never be invited to Heart Palace for tarty tarts! And no, strawberry jam tastes NOTHING like the oh so delicious squigberry jam. Your loss!

The first published edition of ALICE'S ADVENTURES IN WONDERLAND appeared early in July 1865 and featured illustrator John Tenniel's iconic artwork. Alyss now had to adjust to the fact that the betrayal was no longer an unpublished manuscript but an actual book that would soon find its way into the hands and hearts of the literate public.

Friday Afternoon

I closed my eyes so I could see back to Wonderland and began to remember.

Me and Dodgson on the Thames River

I wanted to tell him about the Inventors' Parade and the giant mushrooms that were as tall as ten of London's greatest trees set end to end and the caterpillars who knew everything but only told you what they knew you needed to know, but instead the words that came out were the story of my last day in Wonderland and The Cat and Redd entering the palace and her ear-shattering cries of "Off with their heads!!!"

At this point I opened my eyes and saw poor Mr. Dodgson absolutely pale with fright.

He asked, "What, my dear, is so WONDERFUL about WONDERLAND???" I smiled and told him there was much, MUCH more to tell …

I cannot help but be moved by the beauty of the friendship shared by Charles Lutwidge Dodgson and Alyss Heart. As devastating a betrayal as the eventual outcome may have been, for a period of time two kindred spirits found each other in the same world and proceeded to have a riotous good time. Charles Dodgson was a young mathematics don at Christ Church when he first met the daughters of Dean Liddell and, as history has voluminously recorded, was particularly in awe of the daughter supposedly named "Alice."

CATERPILLAR

"O! that way madness lies; let me shun that." —William Shakespeare

Following the publication of *Princess Alyss of Wonderland*, Dame Agnes received a tip regarding an unusual painting that could be traced back to Buckingham Palace circa. 1872. Upon investigation she discovered these facts:

As an engagement gift, Alice Liddell took up the brush and palette to paint a self-portrait at the request of her fiancé Prince Leopold. The result of her artistic self-examination yielded a strange fractured portrait of someone obviously unsure of who she is and what she wants! Is it child or is it a woman? Is it Alice or is it Alyss? The cubist style precedes that particular art movement by over 30 years. Could it have somehow inspired the painters of the early 20th century? After Alice Liddell's disappearance in the midst of their royal wedding, Prince Leopold disposed of the painting (never having liked it in the first place) which began a circuitous trek across Europe until coming to Malaga, Spain in the year 1881 to hang on the wall of an old school house until now.

Awaiting Verification!
We recently received these three pieces of possible 'Alyss' art from Dame Agnes. All three are from a private collection and are currently on loan to the Institute for forensic testing and authentication. We will have the results of our ongoing Alyss art investigation in geo-graphic novel Hatter M Volume 3.

"No excellent soul is exempt from a mixture of madness." –ARISTOTLE

...GE 46 – SEE ATTACHED SKETCH

...NEL 1 - WIDE – WORM'S EYE VIEW

...e Lovejoy Mansion in flames – see FULL FRONT of house from
...ont porch/veranda to THIRD
...OOR and ROOF where the flames are shooting out. (FLAMES ARE
...CAREY – BUT MINIMAL – THIS HOUSE WILL BE SAVED
...NTACT)

...WE SEE A TIME LAPSE SEQUENCE across the panel as the Hat (via
...3 shots in panel 1) coming from the left side of panel…begins to
...TRANSFORM from NORMAL SIZE HAT to EXPANDING BRIM
...and DEEPENING CROWN – in THIRD PHASE we see the FLAMES
...being 'pulled' TOWARD THE HAT AS IT SPINS ABOVE THE
...HOUSE

2
Hatter leaps from his running horse onto the veranda roof

3 – WIDE - HOUSE ON FIRE
FIRST SECTION - Hatter – utilizing an early Wonderland form of the
popular 'parkour' climbs/leaps from the veranda UPWARD

4
SECOND SECTION – HATTER MOVING VERTICAL – UP TO
THE SECOND STORY

5
THIRD SECTION -- HATTER VERTICAL TO THE THIRD STORY
WHERE ARIEL IS SURROUNDED BY FLAMES AS HAT AGAIN
SPINS PAST – FLAMES 'PULLED AWAY' FROM ARIEL BY HATS
PROPULSION – HATTER PULLS ARIEL INTO HIS ARMS

We want a classic
southern mansion.
This looks good

This is how
we should
show the
progres-
sion

The flames and smoke being
sucked into the Hat should
have more of
a tornado
effect. The
smoke is too
scattered,
looking
more like
a coloring element. It
needs to be over emphasized that
the Hat is sucking up the Flames and
the smoke into a cone-like tornado.
This should also be shown in the last
panel of the page.

The Plantation on fire should
be the main focus of the page.
It needs to be a much bigger
panel and at a more extreme
angle. I liked the cart on
Panel 2 but Hatter' action
is unclear. He needs to look
more like he's jumping. So
show him in a crouch or
diving through the air.

wide of the ballroom in the mansion

rred floors -- only the humanity and energy of the people make it beautiful

GROUND
ays the piano. Hayward plays the fiddle. Ariel and Lulu waltz together around the once
– now scarred and stripped ballroom. Very formal – funny and cute.

GROUND
and Rosalind waltz together. Very formal. Elegant. But there is also something very
nal between them.

ROSALIND
The war has changed our lives forever.
Lovejoy was built by artisans to stand
a thousand years.
If you could only IMAGINE how beautiful this once was…

HATTER
I can…I can imagine it all.

Page layout needs a shake up, a full bleed for the main panel of interest.

INSERT 'IMAGINATION ' PANEL OVER PART OF PANEL 1 – this panel can be a 'bleed'
t progresses (left to right) beginning with Hatter's POV across the page beginning in the grays
d muted colors of Panel 1's REALTY and progressing into the HYPER-REAL WONDER-
AND COLORS AS IT COMES FROM HATTER'S IMAGINATION

atter 'sees' the ballroom transformed and at the main focal point 'sees' Rosalind dressed in a
owing gown – the image is reminiscent of the beauty and fantasy of Wonderland. Rosalind's
air and gown has a Wonderland fantasy to it as do Hatter's imagining of the room, the candelabra
more vivid, surreal than anything Earth could create.

SEE ATTACHED REFERENCE IMAGE OF QUEEN GENEVIEVE FOR ROSALIND 'IMAGI-
NATION' LOOK

NOTE: PANELS 3 AND 4 – BOTTOM OF PAGE – CAN BE POSITIONED OVER THE
IMAGINATION 'BLEED' OF PANEL 2 AS IT SPREADS TOWARD THE BOTTOM OF THE
PAGE

3 – SMALL PANEL
TWO SHOT HATTER AND ROSALIND HEADS CLOSE TOGETHER

ROSALIND
In the South it is considered very
bad manners to ask personal questions of guests…

4 – SMALL PANEL
CLOSE UP – ROSALIND'S EYES BOLD – STARING INTO HATTER'S FACE AT SIDE OF
PANEL

ROSALIND
But I believe   u told me
e from.

Here is Miss Emily's sketch with some changes. Pull back from Rosalind. Take out Wonderland objects behind Rosalind.

"Follow your inner moonlight; don't hide the madness." —ALLEN GINSBERG

Add notes, swirling in Wonderland colors to feel the sweep of the music.

Emphasize the colored glow of Wonderland as reality bleeds into Hatter's vision of Rosalind.

Farewell dear readers,
We leave you with this reassurance
that Hatter always keeps his word!

Madly yours,

The Institute

CHAPTER 8

BOARDERLAND: WONDERLAND'S largest, most powerful neighbor, consisting wholly of nomadic towns and cities,
any one of which might be situated amid the sandy dunes of
Duneraria one week but spread out alongside Bookie River
the next; an uncultivated, expansive place where itiner-
ant settlements had always been separated by large tracts of
unpopulated, rugged terrain; a land where, except for clashes,
tribes used to keep to themselves, allowed to observe their
own customs and rituals so long as they submitted to Arch
as king of *all* Boarderland.

But that was before Arch had been reunited with an
old friend and his practice of perpetuating hostilities among
the tribes revealed for what it was: the method by which
he maintained his authority, stoking animosities so that the

Astacans and Maldoids and others wouldn't unite to form an army his own could not hope to rival.

That was before Redd Heart.

"WILMA was *not* activated as she should've been, but I recognize her effects," the former king whispered to one of his intel ministers, who was crouched behind an orb cannon to avoid notice. "I'm willing to bet Redd is without her powers. We wouldn't be returning to Boarderland if she had them."

"You don't know for sure she's without imagination, my liege."

"Not yet. But I will."

The military caravan had halted in Outerwilderbeastia before the final push back into Boarderland. With the prospect of it before him, the country Arch had so recently ruled suddenly seemed inhospitable and miserly, a dusty landscape of wind-battered tenements and few natural resources. It had never been enough. He didn't want to be king again, not if it meant being king of Boarderland alone.

"Nor can you know if such a loss of imagination is permanent," the intel minister said.

Arch looked off to where Redd lounged beneath a canopy at the edge of the sparring arena, an open space surrounded by tribal warriors and Earth mercenaries. Sitting with Mistress Heart in the shade along with the rest of her top military rank was The Cat—half feline, half Wonderlander, total assassin; and Vollrath, that member of the tutor species devoted to Black Imagination. All unengaged troops had been ordered to gather for a series of brawls. It was supposed to be entertainment.

"You see how Redd pretends to give no thought to the fact that even now," Arch said to his minister, "both in front of us and behind, her recruits are fighting Alyss' forces? She's overacting. With this leisurely retreat of ours, she's trying to prove that clashes with her niece's armies are nothing and she can go where she likes, Wonderland is as good as hers. I don't believe it."

Arch knew Redd's impatience too well: In taking back the crown, in putting an end to Alyss Heart, Redd would never have been leisurely if she could help it.

"Had WILMA wreaked what she was supposed to," the minister said, "Boarderland and Wonderland would already be yours, my liege."

Arch nodded. "If Redd's without her imagination, so is Queen Alyss. I have to take a chance and make my move while they're without their powers."

Shouts rose from the troops around the sparring arena. Hoofs and fists pumped the air. The first brawl had begun.

"Arch!" Redd's voice cut through the cheers and catcalls, her eyes on the former king.

Arch dipped his head, the closest he would ever come to a bow. "Coming, Your Imperial Viciousness!" Turning away to take his position at Redd's side, keeping his lips as still as possible, he told his minister, "You're going to pay a visit to the Glass Eyes' tent and you're going to do and say exactly as I instruct . . ."

~

It could not have been going worse for her niece, chessmen succumbing to slashing blades, card soldiers falling a pack at a time under a barrage of orb generators and cannonball spiders. How invigorated Her Imperial Viciousness had felt, watching Alyss' pathetic defensive maneuvers as Boarderland's twenty-one tribes, under *her* command, stormed into Outerwilderbeastia, each tribe wielding the weapons they most favored: gossamer shots (Awr), mind riders (Maldoids), kill-quills (Scabbler), death-balls (Gnobi), knobkerries (Astacans), and the crude tools of less developed tribes hardly worth her notice. No, her attack on Wonderland couldn't have been going better. Her Boarderlanders and Earth recruits had laid flat shuffle after shuffle of Heart soldiers, rampaging through Outerwilderbeastia into the Everlasting Forest and the Chessboard Desert, converging on Wondertropolis. How she had frowned with appreciation as The Cat swiped claws across the chests of Six Cards and swatted down pawns! How she had grimaced with pride as her foremost military rank, the most gifted of her Earth recruits, proved their worth: Sacrenoir, who raised the bones of the dead into skeleton-zombies desperate to satisfy their insatiable hunger for live flesh; Siren Hecht, unhinging her jaw to release high-pitched screams that sent platoons squirming to the ground in pain; Alistaire Poole, the surgeon/undertaker who conducted autopsies on living card soldiers; and Mr. Van de Skülle, dexterously lashing chessmen with his spike-tipped whip.

And at last she'd been making her way down Heart Boulevard, toward Heart Palace and a final victory over her presumptuous upstart of a niece! But that's when things had gone instantly, horribly—

Odd.

She awoke, lying in the middle of the boulevard, her head hazy, her soldiers splayed about in various stages of unconsciousness. She had tried to view Alyss with her imagination's eye but saw only blackness. Whether or not her niece had harnassed some sort of reserve power from the Heart Crystal, as Arch had suggested, Redd didn't know. The infusion of strength she'd experienced when nearing the Heart Crystal had gone in a moment. She'd been barren of imagination ever since.

"Not bad," she said, applauding listlessly as Ripkins dragged a defeated Glass Eye from the sparring arena.

She had called for the fights in order to boost morale. The tribes were fitful, having never remained in such proximity to one another for any length of time and not understanding why they hadn't stormed Heart Palace when they had been so close. But she couldn't have risked entering the palace when Alyss might have had her powers while she . . . no, she hated to admit it even to herself. Besides giving her an opportunity to observe what Arch's bodyguards were capable of, the sparring matches would distract the troops from their unease.

Redd nodded in Blister's direction. "Your turn."

The bodyguard stepped into the sparring arena, pulled off his elbow-length gloves and placed them neatly in his pocket. Her Imperial Viciousness glared out at the troops.

"Anyone wishing to earn my special regard, which should be every one of you, will step forward and earn it!"

Blister waited for an adversary, but none came forward.

"Are this Doomsine's talents so great that you'd all risk *my* wrath as cowards?"

"Let me fight him."

The Cat's words had come out as a growl. He was standing between Redd and Arch in humanoid form, erect on two heavily muscled legs, his strong arms reaching down past his waist, his paws unsheathing claws sharp and long enough to run through an average-sized Wonderlander. His fangs showed beneath his flat pink nose, his twitching whiskers.

"You've only one life left," Redd reminded him.

"And it's worthless if I don't risk it doing what I do best."

"I like your rashness, feline. Take your position."

The Cat leapt into the sparring arena. He and Blister eyed each other, unmoving.

"Is this supposed to be impressive?" Redd snorted.

Like one warming up for more strenuous exercise, Blister

tossed a whipsnake grenade, but The Cat easily sidestepped its slithering, snapping electric coils. Blister would try to work his way in close, The Cat knew. Every swipe of a paw could prove as deadly to himself as to Blister. He should be careful. But he wasn't here to be careful, so he ran straight at his adversary, his powerful legs carrying him forward with such thrust and purpose that anyone else would have tried to flee, but Blister merely remained where he was.

The Cat pounced—a low, perfectly horizontal leap forward. He morphed into a kitten in mid-air, ducking Blister's outstretched hands, and transformed back into a humanoid as he passed, raking his claws across Blister's shin. He came to a stop three spirit-dane lengths away, a full-formed assassin again.

Blister showed no sign of feeling the bloody gash in his leg. He produced an AD52 from somewhere beneath his coat and held down its trigger, shooting a full deck of razorcards at The Cat and stalking after it. The Cat avoided what projectiles he could and batted down others, smacking the tops of them without touching their sharp edges, but Blister was able to get within arm's reach and—

The Cat hissed, leapt back. Blister had grazed his shoulder with a finger. The fur immediately swelled; the skin underneath it bubbled. The Cat popped the swelling with a claw and spat.

Beneath Redd's canopy, Arch leaned toward his mistress, smiling and flirtatious.

"You're looking particularly grim, Your Imperial Viciousness."

"Flatterer."

"I *was* going to woo you with lies, Redd, but I have to say, the blurriness that's been part of you and The Cat since your return to our world—"

"What of it?"

"I know you said something about its being the result of your unprecedented journey through the Heart Crystal, but . . . well, it's pretty much gone."

Redd crinkled her nose in what was supposed to be a teasing manner. "Again I ask: What of it, Archy? Does it surprise you that I used my powerful imagination to rid myself of a loathsome blurriness? It's just taken longer than I'd liked. What the Heart Crystal gives isn't so easily done away with . . . even for me."

"Hm," Arch said.

Blister and The Cat stood breathing heavily in the middle of the sparring arena, each waiting for the other to make the next move. Blister's clothes were shredded, thin lines of blood showing where The Cat's claws had dragged across his chest, back, leg, and arms. The Cat's shoulder and forearms were leaking—wherever Blister had even lightly touched him, yellow pus dribbled from popped bubbles of skin.

"Caterpillar," Vollrath noted, his ashen finger pointing at a series of green smoke rings drifting out from behind a fried dormouse hawker's stall.

In the sparring arena, Blister threw a dagger at The Cat. The feline dropped into a crouch, about to spring forward.

"Enough!" Redd shouted. "As much as we're all dying to see the outcome of this little dalliance, I may still have use for *both* of you."

Though she'd always deemed caterpillar-oracles to be ugly, annoying creatures, Her Imperial Viciousness stomped toward the dormouse hawker's stall, leaving Blister and The Cat to believe they had lost their sole chance to prove which of them was the greater fighter. They couldn't know there would soon be another.

AUTOMATIC PICTURES
PUBLISHING

5225 Wilshire Blvd. Suite 525
Los Angeles, CA 90036

info@lookingglasswars.com
automaticstudio@gmail.com

www.lookingglasswars.com
www.cardsoldierwars.com

If you have probing questions
that you would like answered,
please email us at
info@lookingglasswars.com